I0720882

Black Eyed Children Encounters

Created By Angel Hepburn

All Stories are works of fiction

Black-eyed children or black-eyed kids, in American contemporary legend, are paranormal creatures that resemble children between ages 6 and 16, with pale skin and black eyes, who are reportedly seen hitchhiking or begging, or are encountered on doorsteps of residential homes.

From Wikipedia

Table Of Contents

Encounter 1

Sarah

Sarah jolted awake in the dead of night, her heart pounding as if it wanted to escape her chest. She blinked, trying to make sense of her surroundings, only to freeze in terror as her eyes focused on two figures standing motionless at the foot of her bed. They were children, or at least they appeared to be, but there was something profoundly wrong with them.

Their eyes, empty and void of any color, stared back at her with an intensity that sent shivers down her spine. The room seemed to darken around them, as if their presence alone was draining the very life from the air. Sarah's breath caught in her throat as a suffocating sense of dread filled the room.

Fear held her captive, preventing her from screaming or even moving. The children remained eerily silent, their small bodies shrouded in shadows. Their pale skin seemed to glow faintly,

accentuating the darkness that consumed them.
Sarah's mind struggled to comprehend what she
was seeing. Who were these children? And why
were they in her bedroom?

The air grew heavy, laden with an
unexplainable malevolence that permeated the
atmosphere. It was as if an invisible force pressed
against her, crushing her spirit, while her thoughts
swirled in a whirlwind of panic and confusion. She
desperately wanted to escape, to flee from this
nightmare, but her body felt paralyzed, rooted to
the bed.

A voice, barely a whisper, hissed inside
Sarah's mind, bypassing her ears and filling her
thoughts with an unnerving message. "Let us in," it
cooed, icy tendrils of fear snaking around her
consciousness. The voice was neither male nor
female, but seemed to carry the weight of centuries,
resonating with an ancient darkness.

Sarah's mind raced, trying to resist the
insidious command that beckoned her to surrender.

Her instincts screamed for her to resist, to fight against whatever evil force these children represented. But her willpower faltered as a morbid curiosity began to gnaw at her resolve. She found herself entertaining the thought, however briefly, of opening the door to something beyond comprehension.

With an effort of will, she managed to summon a shaky voice, trembling with equal parts fear and defiance. "Who... who are you?" she stammered, her voice barely audible in the thick silence that hung in the room.

The children's gazes intensified, the depths of their eyes expanding into an abyss that threatened to swallow her whole. They spoke in unison, their voices harmonizing in a chilling symphony of darkness. "We are the Forgotten Ones," they whispered, their words resonating through Sarah's very being.

Sarah's body convulsed with a mixture of terror and fascination. The Forgotten Ones. The words echoed in her mind, etching themselves onto her soul like a forbidden incantation. She could feel her resolve wavering, her resistance crumbling under their unearthly presence.

But just as she was about to succumb to the alluring whispers, a surge of determination coursed through her veins. With a newfound strength, Sarah mustered every ounce of defiance she had left. "No," she cried out, her voice filled with newfound resolve. "You cannot have me!"

As if struck by an invisible force, the children recoiled, their eyes widening momentarily before they dissolved into shadows, disappearing from Sarah's sight. The room brightened, the weight of dread lifting from her chest, leaving her gasping for air.

Sarah collapsed back onto her bed, her body trembling with the aftershocks of the encounter. She knew that whatever had just transpired, it was not a mere dream. The memory of those Black-Eyed Children and their haunting presence would forever be etched in her mind, a chilling reminder that there are forces lurking in the darkness, waiting for the moment to seize upon the vulnerable.

From that night on, Sarah vowed to remain vigilant, guarding herself against the unknown. She had faced the Forgotten Ones and survived, but she knew she would never truly be free of the lingering darkness that had invaded her life.

Encounter 2

Lisa

Lisa sat at the hotel reception desk, her eyes growing heavy with exhaustion. It had been a long night, filled with demanding guests and the weight of responsibility. The clock ticked closer to the early morning hours, signaling the end of her shift. Just a few more minutes, she thought, and then she could finally retreat to the solace of her own bed.

As the last guest checked out, the hotel lobby fell into an eerie silence. Lisa glanced around, the dim lighting casting long shadows across the deserted space. With a sigh of relief, she closed the reception area and headed upstairs to the empty rooms.

Stepping onto the fourth floor, Lisa's footsteps echoed in the corridor, a hollow sound that seemed to magnify her isolation. She reached the end of the hallway and pulled out the master key, preparing to make a final check of the rooms before retiring for the night.

She opened the first door, peeking inside to ensure everything was in order. The room was vacant, its stillness broken only by the faint hum of the air conditioning. Lisa moved methodically from room to room, her senses on high alert despite her weariness.

As she approached the last room on the floor, a sudden chill raced down her spine. A foreboding presence seemed to emanate from within, and she hesitated, her hand hovering over the doorknob. Something was wrong—she could feel it in her bones.

Summoning her courage, Lisa pushed the door open, revealing a dimly lit room. The air felt thick and heavy, suffused with an otherworldly energy that made her skin crawl. She stepped inside, her heart pounding in her chest.
In the corner of the room, a figure stood, barely discernible in the darkness. As Lisa's eyes

adjusted, she recoiled in horror. It was a child, or at least it appeared to be, but its eyes—those soulless, black orbs—sent a wave of terror crashing over her.

The Black-Eyed Child stared at her, its gaze penetrating her very soul. The room seemed to pulse with a malevolent energy, as if the air itself was tainted by the presence of this unearthly being. Lisa's breath caught in her throat, and she struggled to break free from the grip of fear that held her rooted to the spot.

With a voice that seemed to reverberate within her mind, the Black-Eyed Child whispered, its words laced with a dark promise. "Come with me," it hissed, its voice dripping with menace. "Embrace the darkness that awaits. Unspeakable horrors shall be your eternal companion."

The whispered words echoed in Lisa's mind, their insidious tendrils worming their way into her thoughts. Images of unimaginable nightmares flashed before her eyes, her own sanity teetering on the precipice of madness.

But a flicker of resistance sparked within Lisa's spirit. She refused to succumb to the child's wicked allure. Summoning every ounce of willpower, she managed to find her voice, trembling yet defiant. "No," she gasped, her words a defiant declaration. "I will not be lured into darkness. You hold no power over me."

The Black-Eyed Child recoiled, its form flickering in the dim light. A mixture of anger and frustration flashed across its face before it vanished, leaving Lisa standing alone in the haunted room.

As the door slammed shut behind her, Lisa staggered back, her heart pounding in her chest. The encounter had left an indelible mark on her psyche, its chilling presence forever etched into her memory. The whispered words still echoed in her mind, a haunting reminder of the unspeakable horrors she had narrowly escaped.

From that night forward, Lisa carried the weight of that encounter, a constant reminder of the darkness that lurked beyond the veil of reality. She knew she had been fortunate, but she also knew that the Black-Eyed Child's words would forever be etched in her consciousness, a haunting reminder of the terrors that could have consumed her soul.

Encounter 3

John

John's tired eyes strained to focus on the empty road ahead as he drove through the desolate countryside, his mind yearning for the comfort of his own bed. It was late at night, and the darkness outside enveloped the world, amplifying his weariness. The only sound that filled the air was the hum of his car's engine.

As he rounded a bend, his headlights pierced through the night, revealing two small figures standing by the roadside. John's heart skipped a beat, and a knot tightened in his stomach. He slowed down, his curiosity mingling with caution.

The two figures, barely visible in the dim light, stepped closer to the car. Panic fluttered in John's chest as their features became discernible. They were children, their faces partially obscured by shadows. But it was their eyes—dark and soulless—that sent a chill coursing through his veins.

The Black-Eyed Children approached the car, their gazes fixed on John, unblinking and void of emotion. An overwhelming sense of unease washed over him, an instinctual warning that these children were not what they appeared to be.

A tremor of fear threaded its way through his thoughts as one of the children tapped on the car window. John hesitated, his hand gripping the steering wheel tightly. Their pleas, barely audible, reached his ears like distant whispers on the wind.

"Please," one of them murmured, their voice devoid of inflection, "let us in. We need your help."

The words hung heavy in the air, their unsettling plea seeping into John's consciousness. His instincts screamed at him to drive away, to escape from this unnatural encounter, but a morbid curiosity held him captive. Against his better judgment, he lowered the window slightly, a sliver of apprehension mingling with a desire to understand.

"Why do you need my help?" John asked, his voice betraying a mix of trepidation and intrigue. The children's eyes glowed with an eerie intensity as they spoke in unison, their voices blending together in a disconcerting harmony. "Our home is gone. We need shelter. Let us into your car."

Their words sent shivers down John's spine. The sense of danger escalated, as if the very air surrounding them had grown colder and more oppressive. He couldn't shake the feeling that letting them in would unleash a malevolence beyond comprehension.

Summoning his courage, John forced himself to deny their request. "I'm sorry, but I can't help you," he replied, his voice trembling. "I need to keep going."

A flicker of anger passed across the children's faces, their facade slipping for a moment, revealing a glimpse of something far more sinister. But just as quickly, their expressions returned to a blank slate, the façade of innocence restored.

"Very well," they replied in unison, their voices taking on an icy tone. "But remember, traveler, there are fates far worse than death."

With that chilling warning, the children slowly receded into the darkness, their haunting gazes fixed on John until they were swallowed by the night. The weight of their presence lingered in the car, a lingering reminder of the narrow escape John had just experienced.

His heart racing, John pressed on the gas pedal, eager to put as much distance as possible between himself and those haunting figures. The encounter had left an indelible mark on his soul, a reminder that there were forces beyond his understanding, lurking in the shadows, waiting for the chance to ensnare unwary souls.

As he drove into the night, John couldn't shake the feeling that their words held a truth he dared not fully comprehend. The memory of those

Black-Eyed Children, their emotionless eyes etched into his mind, would forever haunt his dreams, a chilling reminder of the horrors that existed just beyond the edge of his reality.

Encounter 4

Daniel

Daniel trudged through the thick mud, his boots sinking with each step as he made his way toward the barn. It was a cold and desolate evening, the moon obscured by heavy clouds that threatened to unleash a storm. He could sense a restlessness in the air, an unease that seemed to permeate the entire farm.

As he approached the barn, the sounds of agitated animals reached his ears—a cacophony of panicked bleats and distressed mooing. His heart skipped a beat, and a knot tightened in his gut. Something was terribly wrong.

With trepidation, Daniel pushed open the creaky barn door, his eyes scanning the dimly lit interior. The air inside was heavy and suffocating, the scent of hay mixed with an acrid undertone. He flicked on the light switch, illuminating the space and revealing the chaos within.

His livestock—normally docile and calm—were in a frenzy. Cows thrashed against their pens, their eyes wide with terror. Horses stomped and whinnied, their muscles tense and their manes disheveled. The usually serene barn had transformed into a scene of wild panic.

As Daniel moved deeper into the barn, a chilling presence brushed against his senses. His gaze fell upon a corner of the structure, where a small figure stood, partially hidden in the shadows. It was a child, but there was something profoundly unsettling about its appearance. Its eyes, void of color and life, stared at Daniel with an intensity that sent a shiver down his spine.

The Black-Eyed Child seemed to emanate an aura of darkness, an energy that unsettled both man and beast. Daniel's instincts screamed at him to flee, to leave this malevolent presence behind, but a grim determination rooted him in place. He needed to protect his animals, to understand the cause of their distress.

"Who are you?" Daniel's voice quivered with a mixture of fear and defiance, his words breaking the oppressive silence.

The child's lips curled into a malevolent smile, revealing rows of unnaturally sharp teeth. Its voice, soft and ethereal, slithered into Daniel's mind. "They fear me," it whispered, its voice echoing with a chilling resonance. "They know what I am, what I can do."

Daniel's heart pounded in his chest, a mixture of anger and protectiveness surging through his veins. He refused to let this entity harm his livelihood. Summoning every ounce of courage, he stepped forward, his voice laced with determination. "Leave this place! You have no power over us!"

As Daniel spoke those words, a surge of defiant energy radiated from him, filling the barn with a burst of light. The Black-Eyed Child recoiled, its form flickering like a candle in the wind. With a final glare, it dissipated into the shadows, leaving a lingering sense of unease in its wake.

Gradually, the agitated animals began to calm down, their panicked cries subsiding. The oppressive atmosphere that had plagued the barn lifted, as if the very air had been cleansed. Daniel knew that the encounter was far from forgotten, but for now, his farm was safe.

He remained vigilant, mindful of the darkness that still lurked at the edges of his existence. The memory of the Black-Eyed Child and its impact on his animals would forever be etched in his mind, a reminder that evil could manifest itself in the most unexpected places.

As he closed the barn door behind him, Daniel vowed to protect his farm and all that resided within it. He would remain ever watchful, knowing that the forces of darkness were always waiting for a chance to intrude upon his world.

Encounter 5

Jake

Jake gripped the steering wheel tightly as he barreled down the desolate highway, the monotonous hum of the engine lulling him into a state of weary concentration. The road stretched out before him, a seemingly endless ribbon cutting through the barren landscape.

As he rounded a bend, his tired eyes caught sight of a figure standing on the side of the road. A chill ran down Jake's spine, his foot instinctively easing o the accelerator. There, in the dim glow of his headlights, stood a child. But it was no ordinary child.

The Black-Eyed Child stared at him with those empty, soulless eyes, a sense of unease seeping into Jake's bones. The air around him grew thick and heavy, as if a foreboding presence had descended upon the highway. His instincts screamed at him to keep driving, to leave this

unnatural encounter behind, but a curiosity mixed with fear compelled him to stop.
With a trembling hand, Jake pulled the truck to a halt, the engine grumbling to a halt. Silence enveloped the cabin, save for the faint rustle of wind against the windows. His heart pounded in his chest as he watched the child slowly approach his vehicle.

As the child drew nearer, a profound stillness settled over the highway. Jake's breath caught in his throat, his mind racing to make sense of the inexplicable. How could a child be out here alone, in the dead of night, miles away from civilization? The Black-Eyed Child reached the driver's side window, its gaze fixed upon Jake. Its voice, soft and haunting, resonated within his mind. "Help me," it whispered, the words laced with an otherworldly charm. "Let me in. I can take away your pain."

A surge of panic coursed through Jake's veins, mingling with a strange allure emanating from the child's words. His rational mind fought against the strange temptation, warning him of the unknown horrors that lurked beneath the surface. Yet, an inexplicable longing for relief from his burdens gnawed at his resolve.

"No," Jake managed to choke out, his voice quivering with a mix of fear and defiance. "I won't let you in."

The child's expression contorted, a flicker of anger crossing its face before returning to its eerily serene facade. "Your choice," it replied, its voice now tinged with a hint of menace. "But remember, there are consequences to denying me."

With that, the Black-Eyed Child vanished into the darkness, leaving Jake alone in his stalled truck, his heart pounding in his chest. As he desperately tried to restart the engine, an overwhelming sense of dread settled upon him.

Hours passed, but the truck remained stubbornly silent. Jake's mind raced with visions of the horrors that awaited him, the consequences of denying the Black-Eyed Child's request. The desolate highway transformed into a prison of his own making, the weight of his decision bearing down upon him.

As the first light of dawn crept over the horizon, a tow truck arrived to rescue Jake. But the encounter with the Black-Eyed Child had left an indelible mark on his soul. The memory of those empty, black eyes and the whispered promises lingered, a haunting reminder of the darkness that exists just beyond the edge of perception.

From that day forward, Jake carried the burden of his encounter, forever changed by the chilling presence that had infiltrated his life. The stall of his truck served as a constant reminder that some forces are beyond comprehension, and the consequences of crossing their path can be unfathomable.

Encounter 6

Howard

Howard sat in his dimly lit living room, surrounded by books and articles that debunked the supernatural. He prided himself on his skepticism, finding comfort in the rational explanations for seemingly inexplicable phenomena. The stories of Black-Eyed Children were nothing more than urban legends to him, a figment of the collective imagination.

But one night, as he sat alone in his home, a knock echoed through the stillness. Howard's brows furrowed in confusion. Who could be visiting at this late hour? He approached the door cautiously, his skepticism firmly in place.

As he swung the door open, his eyes widened in surprise. There, standing on his porch, was a child with eyes as dark as the night. The Black-Eyed Child stared at him, its gaze unwavering. A mischievous smile curled upon its lips.

Howard's initial shock gave way to a mix of curiosity and a desire to prove his skepticism right. He invited the child inside, a sense of self-assuredness guiding his actions. This would be an opportunity to expose the hoax, to confront the illusion head-on.

As the Black-Eyed Child stepped across the threshold, a palpable shift in the atmosphere engulfed the house. The air grew heavy, suffocating Howard's lungs. His confidence wavered, but he refused to let fear consume him.

But soon, strange occurrences began to unfold. Objects moved of their own accord, floating through the air before crashing to the ground. Whispers, disembodied and chilling, echoed through the halls. Shadows danced and twisted, taking on sinister forms.

Howard's skepticism crumbled before his eyes, replaced by a gnawing terror that crawled up his spine. He tried to maintain his composure, to rationalize the unexplainable, but the evidence of the supernatural overwhelmed him.

Sleep became a distant memory as nightmares invaded his nights, vivid and tormenting. The Black-Eyed Child's presence seemed to seep into every corner of his home, infiltrating his thoughts and unraveling his sanity. Paranoia consumed him, each creak of the floorboards and flicker of light fueling his mounting dread.

Desperate for answers, Howard delved into the world of the occult and ancient lore, hoping to find a way to banish the dark presence from his home. But every attempt to rid himself of the child's influence only seemed to intensify the haunting phenomena.

Days turned into a blur of fear and exhaustion, Howard's once skeptical mind now teetering on the precipice of madness. The Black-Eyed Child's malevolent influence seemed unrelenting, a force that revealed in his torment.

In a last-ditch e ort, Howard sought the help of a seasoned paranormal investigator. Together, they performed rituals and incantations, hoping to break the grip of the supernatural presence that had ensnared his home.

As the final words of the incantation echoed through the room, the atmosphere shifted once again. The house grew still, the shadows retreating to their rightful places. The Black-Eyed Child, its eyes now devoid of their haunting darkness, vanished, leaving Howard to confront the aftermath of his harrowing encounter.

Though the Black-Eyed Child was gone, the scars it had left upon Howard's psyche remained. The skeptic had been forced to confront the unimaginable, and the fragility of his beliefs had been shattered. The unexplainable had become an inescapable truth, forever etched in his mind, a reminder that there are forces beyond comprehension, lurking in the shadows, waiting to challenge even the staunchest of skeptics.

Encounter 7

Michael

Captain Michael sat in the cockpit of the airplane, his eyes focused on the instruments before him. The plane hummed with a steady rhythm as it soared through the night sky. He glanced out at the vast expanse of darkness, comforted by the familiar solitude of the cockpit.

Suddenly, a flicker of movement caught his attention. Michael's eyes darted to the cabin through the small window separating him from the passengers. He froze in his seat, his heart skipping a beat. A figure stood in the aisle—a child, with eyes as black as the abyss.

Dread washed over him as he realized the impossibility of the situation. How had someone managed to enter the cabin without his knowledge? He radioed the flight attendants, but no response came. A sinking feeling settled in the pit of his stomach. Something was terribly wrong.

Summoning his courage, Michael unbuckled his seatbelt and cautiously stepped out of the cockpit, making his way toward the cabin. The figure stood motionless, its gaze fixed upon him. As he approached, the child's presence seemed to fill the air with an unnerving energy, su ocating and heavy.

"Who are you?" Michael's voice trembled, his hand instinctively reaching for the intercom button to alert the flight attendants. But before he could make a move, a chilling silence enveloped the cabin. The child's eyes bore into his soul, devoid of any emotion.

A series of inexplicable malfunctions rippled through the airplane. The hum of the engines faltered, and the cabin lights flickered ominously. The control panel before Michael blinked with erratic warnings and errors. Panic surged through him as he fought to regain control of the aircraft. With every passing moment, the situation grew more dire. The plane shook violently, as if in the grip of some invisible force. The passengers, unaware of the supernatural presence among them, began to cry out in fear and confusion.

Desperation fueled Michael's actions as he fought against the relentless onslaught of chaos. Sweat dripped down his forehead as he struggled to stabilize the plane. The Black-Eyed Child watched with an unsettling calmness, its mere presence draining his resolve.

As the airplane teetered on the brink of disaster, Michael's mind raced. How could he defeat something beyond the realms of logic and reason? With a surge of determination, he made a fateful decision. He would confront the child head-on, hoping to sever the dark influence that gripped the aircraft.

Summoning every ounce of courage, he approached the Black-Eyed Child, his voice laced with a mixture of defiance and desperation. "Leave this plane! Release us from your grasp!"

A sinister smile curled upon the child's lips, a silent acknowledgment of the havoc it had wrought. With an ethereal whisper, it spoke, its voice echoing through the cabin, "You cannot escape the darkness. It is too late."

But Michael refused to accept defeat. He channeled his inner strength and resilience, drawing upon the years of training and experience that had shaped him into a pilot. With an unyielding will, he fought against the malevolent force that had infiltrated his aircraft.

As the cabin plunged into darkness, a surge of light erupted from within Michael, illuminating the plane. The Black-Eyed Child recoiled, its form flickering and fading, succumbing to the force of Michael's unwavering determination.

Gradually, the malfunctions subsided, and the plane stabilized. The passengers, unaware of the near catastrophe they had narrowly escaped, found themselves bathed in a renewed sense of calm.

But for Michael, the encounter with the Black-Eyed Child would forever haunt him. The memory of its eerie presence, the sensation of being on the precipice of doom, lingered in his mind, a chilling reminder of the darkness that lurks in the most unexpected places.

From that day forward, he knew that some secrets defy explanation, that there are forces beyond comprehension. As he guided the plane safely to its destination, he vowed to carry the weight of his encounter, forever vigilant against the unknown terrors that may lurk in the shadows of the skies.

Encounter 8

Anna

Anna sat at her desk, the remnants of the day's lessons scattered before her. The classroom was empty, the faint echo of children's laughter a distant memory. The fading daylight filtered through the windows, casting long shadows across the room.

As she busied herself with paperwork, a shiver crawled up Anna's spine. An unexplained chill filled the air, and the hairs on the back of her neck stood on end. Something was amiss. She turned slowly, her gaze scanning the room, and her breath caught in her throat.

Standing in the far corner of the classroom was a child, its presence unmistakable. The Black-Eyed Child stood motionless, its eyes devoid of light, its gaze fixed on Anna. The unsettling stillness filled the room, suffocating her with an overwhelming sense of dread.

Fear clutched at Anna's heart, freezing her in place. Her mind raced, desperately seeking an explanation for the impossible sight before her. How had this child entered her classroom undetected? What did it want?

She tried to speak, to call out for help, but her voice betrayed her. It was as if the very presence of the Black-Eyed Child had stolen her ability to utter a single word. Panic coursed through her veins, mingling with a deep sense of helplessness.

As she attempted to move, her body felt heavy, as if invisible chains held her captive. The Black-Eyed Child took a step forward, its gaze never wavering. Its presence exuded a malevolent energy that seemed to seep into every corner of the room. Anna's mind raced with terror, her thoughts spiraling into a chaotic abyss. She desperately sought an escape, but the room seemed to constrict around her, closing o all avenues of retreat. It was as if she was trapped in a nightmare from which there was no waking.

The Black-Eyed Child slid closer, its footsteps silent against the tiled floor. Anna's heart pounded in her chest, a drumbeat of terror. The child's eyes, empty and all-consuming, bore into her soul, tearing at the fabric of her sanity.

A strange whisper filled the air, barely audible yet resonating with an otherworldly power. "Stay with me," the child murmured, its voice a chilling melody that echoed through Anna's mind. "Stay and witness the true depths of darkness." The room seemed to darken, the shadows lengthening and twisting into grotesque shapes. A wave of despair washed over Anna, threatening to drown her in an ocean of fear. She struggled against the invisible restraints, fighting for control of her own body, for her very survival.

In a final surge of defiance, Anna summoned every ounce of strength within her. She closed her eyes, blocking out the horrifying sight before her, and focused on breaking free from the paralyzing grip of the Black-Eyed Child. With a forceful exhale, she opened her eyes, her gaze unyielding. The child recoiled, its form flickering and fading like smoke in the wind. A sudden rush of energy surged through Anna, propelling her forward. She sprinted toward the classroom door, her heart pounding in her chest, her determination overriding the lingering fear.

As she burst through the doorway, the classroom returned to its familiar, empty state. The Black-Eyed Child was gone, vanished into the shadows from whence it came. Anna stood in the hallway, gasping for breath, her body drenched in perspiration. She had escaped the clutches of the dark entity, but the memory of its chilling presence would forever haunt her.

From that day forward, Anna carried the weight of her encounter, forever changed by the encounter with the Black-Eyed Child. The veil of safety and normalcy had been lifted, revealing the hidden terrors that can lurk in the most mundane places. And as she returned to her classroom each day, she remained ever watchful, knowing that sometimes, the darkness can find a way to seep into even the most familiar of spaces.

Encounter 9

Eric

Eric had always cherished the peace and solitude of his suburban home. Nestled in a quiet neighborhood, it was his sanctuary from the chaos of the outside world. But one fateful night, everything changed.

As midnight approached, a soft tapping sound caught Eric's attention. Puzzled, he rose from his comfortable armchair and made his way to the front door. Peering through the peephole, he saw two children standing on his porch, their eyes as black as the night.

A shiver ran down his spine as he recognized them as the Black-Eyed Children, the stories of their eerie presence flashing through his mind. Their emotionless gazes sent a chill through his entire being.

Summoning his courage, Eric opened the door slightly, the safety chain preventing full access. His voice trembled as he spoke, "Can I help you?"

The children stared back at him, their black eyes seemingly devoid of life. Their voices, soft and unnerving, whispered in unison, "Let us in. We need to use your phone."

A surge of unease washed over Eric. He knew better than to grant them entry, his instincts screaming at him to keep them outside. A sense of danger emanated from the children, and he couldn't ignore the warning signs.
"I'm sorry, but I can't help you," Eric replied, his voice laced with apprehension.

The Black-Eyed Children's expressions remained unchanged, but their persistence grew. They begged, their voices desperate and unsettling, their insistence escalating. But Eric stood his ground, refusing to be swayed by their pleas.

After what felt like an eternity, the children finally relented. Their faces twisted into unsettling smiles, their black eyes never wavering. With a final chilling whisper, they turned and vanished into the night.

Relief washed over Eric as he closed the door, securing it with trembling hands. But his sense of safety had been shattered. He couldn't shake the feeling that something terrible had just transpired, that the Black-Eyed Children's presence had left a mark on his life.

The following morning, Eric inspected his front door, his heart sinking as he discovered deep scratch marks etched into the wood. Each mark seemed to hold a sinister message, a warning of the darkness that had sought to invade his home.

The scratches became a haunting reminder, etched into his psyche. Sleep eluded him as nightmares plagued his nights, visions of the Black-Eyed Children seeking entry, their malevolent presence lurking just beyond his doorstep.

Days turned into weeks, and the lingering sense of dread consumed Eric's every waking moment. He felt constantly watched, as if the children's eyes were still fixed upon him, even in the safety of his own home.

His once tranquil abode transformed into a fortress of paranoia. Every creak and rustle sent him into a state of heightened alertness. He reinforced his doors and windows, his home now a prison against an unknown threat.

But the fear remained, festering within him like a dark stain on his soul. The scratch marks on his door were a constant reminder of the horror he had encountered, a chilling testament to the Black-Eyed Children's persistence.

Eric's life became a relentless pursuit of normalcy, a desperate attempt to outrun the haunting memories. Yet, deep down, he knew that the children's visit was not the end. Their dark presence loomed in the shadows, a specter of dread that refused to be forgotten.

As time passed, Eric became a recluse, withdrawing from the world. His once vibrant spirit was overshadowed by a perpetual state of anxiety. The scratch marks served as a constant reminder of his vulnerability, a reminder that the Black-Eyed Children could return at any moment.

Though others may dismiss his fear as irrational, Eric knew the truth. The Black-Eyed Children had left their mark, not just on his door but on his very soul. And as he lived in the shadow of their presence, he vowed to remain vigilant, forever haunted by the possibility of their return.

Encounter 10

Robert

Robert had always been drawn to the mysteries of the supernatural, fascinated by the unexplained and the realms beyond human comprehension. When he heard the rumors of a haunted forest where Black-Eyed Children had been sighted, he felt an irresistible pull to investigate.

Armed with a flashlight and a camera, Robert ventured into the heart of the forest, its ancient trees towering above him like silent sentinels. The air was heavy with an eerie stillness, broken only by the rustling of leaves and his own racing heartbeat.

As he delved deeper into the forest, the atmosphere grew thick with a sense of foreboding. Shadows danced among the trees, and whispers seemed to echo in the wind. But Robert pressed on, undeterred by the chilling aura that surrounded him.

Suddenly, the sound of giggling filled the air. It was soft and haunting, like the laughter of lost souls. Robert's senses went on high alert as he scanned his surroundings, his flashlight sweeping the area. Yet, he saw nothing—only the inky darkness of the forest.

Undeterred, he continued his exploration, his curiosity overriding his growing unease. But the giggles persisted, growing louder and more unsettling with each step. The children's laughter seemed to come from all directions, bouncing o the trees and resonating within Robert's mind. His heart pounded in his chest as he approached a small clearing. In the dim light, he caught a glimpse of movement—a fleeting figure, small and shadowy. The Black-Eyed Children had revealed themselves.

Frozen with a mixture of fear and fascination, Robert watched as the children materialized before him. Their eyes were pools of emptiness, absorbing the feeble light of his flashlight. The eerie giggles echoed through the air, piercing his soul with their chilling melody.

Without warning, the children vanished, disappearing into the inky blackness of the forest. Their sudden disappearance left Robert shaken to his core, his heart racing, and his mind racing to comprehend the inexplicable.

Determined to capture evidence of the encounter, Robert raised his camera, snapping photos into the darkness. But as he reviewed the images, he was met with disappointment. The photographs were blurred and distorted, as if the Black-Eyed Children had defied capture, leaving only ethereal traces behind.

Night after night, Robert relived the encounter in his dreams. The giggles haunted his every waking moment, their ghostly echoes etched into his mind. He became consumed by the need to understand the truth behind the Black-Eyed Children, to uncover the secrets they held.

His quest for answers led him to delve even deeper into the realm of the paranormal, researching ancient legends and consulting with experts. Yet, the mystery of the Black-Eyed Children remained elusive, their origins and intentions hidden in the depths of darkness.

Haunted by their giggles, Robert became a prisoner of his own obsession. He withdrew from the world, his every waking moment consumed by the enigma that had swallowed him whole. The forest had taken its toll, leaving him a changed man, forever marked by the encounter with the Black-Eyed Children.

In the depths of night, he would still hear their eerie laughter, a constant reminder of the supernatural forces that lurked just beyond the veil of reality. And though his search for answers continued, Robert knew that some mysteries were never meant to be unraveled, and the Black-Eyed Children would forever remain a haunting enigma.

The Grimoire of Nightmares
Black Eyed Children Encounters

In this installment of The Grimoire of Nightmares series, delve into ten gripping tales that revolve around eerie encounters with enigmatic entities known as the black-eyed children. These paranormal beings bear an uncanny resemblance to children aged between 6 and 16, donning pale complexions and haunting black eyes. Their presence is often associated with hitchhiking, panhandling, or unsettling doorstep encounters at residential homes. While skeptics dismiss their existence as mere fiction, there are those who claim firsthand experiences with these enigmatic figures. Regardless of your beliefs, these chilling encounters are bound to leave you cautiously checking your locks and hesitating to answer late-night door knocks. Above all, remember this vital warning: **never, under any circumstances, invite them in!**

www.ingramcontent.com/pod-product-compliance
Lightning Source LLC
Chambersburg PA
CBHW042035180726
48295CB00006B/108